2014

What is a Friend?

What is a Friend?

By Etan Boritzer   Illustrated by Jeff Vernon

Third Printing 2014

VLB *Veronica Lane Books*

www.veronicalanebooks.com email: etan@veronicalanebooks.com
2554 Lincoln Blvd. Ste 142, Los Angeles, CA 90291 USA
Tel/Fax: +1 (800) 651-1001 / Intl: +1 (310) 745-0162

Library of Congress Cataloging-In-Publication Data
Boritzer, Etan, 1950-
What Is a Friend / by Etan Boritzer
Illustrated by Jeff Vernon -- 1st Edition
p. cm.

SUMMARY: Presents children with an understanding of the dynamics of interpersonal relationships.

Audience: Grades K - 5

ISBN: 978-0976243-8-4 (Hardbound)
ISBN: 978-0976243-9-1 (Paperback)

The Library of Congress No.2008935793

The Institute on Violence, Abuse and Trauma's mission, in collaboration with Alliant University, San Diego, is to provide a comprehensive information resource, professional training and research center. In order to improve the quality of life and care for all those affected by violence, abuse, and trauma IVAT works on local, national and international scales.

Founded in 1984 by Dr. Robert Geffner, the nationally acclaimed Family Violence and Sexual Assault Institute (FVSAI) was combined into IVAT in 2005. The Institute's vision is a world free of violence, abuse and trauma.

www.ivatcenters.org

IVAT is a non-profit 501(c)3 organization

...to the children of the world...

What is a friend?

What does a friend look like?
What does a friend sound like?

How does a friend act?
How does a friend *not* act?

Maybe a friend is not just about
the stuff we see
on the outside of a person,
but maybe a friend
is more about the stuff
on the *inside* of a person.

What does a friend look like inside?

What is a friend?

Maybe a friend is somebody
you can play with,
and be yourself with,
or just laugh and act silly with,
or just kind of hang out together with.

Maybe a friend is somebody
who can help you
if you have a problem —
and maybe a friend is somebody
who *you* can help
if they have a problem.

Maybe a friend is somebody
you can trust not to make you cry,
and trust not to hurt you on purpose.

But if a friend hurts you,
can he or she still be your friend?

What *is* a friend?

Does a friend yell at you?

Maybe you are going to cross the street
without looking, and a car is coming —
should your friend yell at you, *Hey, watch out!*

Maybe you are going to do something
that is not right —
should your friend yell at you
before you do it?

What if you yell at your friend
to protect him or her from doing something
that is not right,
but what if your friend doesn't listen to you —
should you still be friends?

What do you have to do
to have a friend?

Do you have to act funny
to have a friend?

Do you have to wear cool clothes
to have a friend?

Do you have to give presents and stuff
to have a friend?

Do you have to like everything about somebody
to have a friend?

Do you have to be bossed around
to have a friend?

Maybe sometimes we have to think hard
about what we will or won't do
to have a friend.

Maybe a friend is somebody
that you can share stuff with.

Maybe you can share
some popcorn at the movies
with a friend.

Maybe you can share
your favorite video game,
or favorite clothes
with a friend.

Maybe if you are worried
or scared about something,
you can share your worst fear
or an important secret
with a friend.

Maybe if your friend is sick,
or gets hurt, or if your friend is unhappy,
maybe you can share some time
with a friend.

Sharing is a really important part
of having a friend!

Can you say *No!* to a friend?

Can you say *No!* to a friend
who is always being pushy
and trying to take over.

Can you say *No!* to a friend
who plays rough like a bully,
and maybe hurts people.

Can you say *No!* to a friend
who uses bad words,
or lies about stuff,
or says nasty things about other people.

Can you say *No!* to a friend
who wants you to do stuff
that you don't want to do.

And if you say *No!* to a friend
and your friend doesn't change,
what can you do about it?

When is a friend *not* a friend?

Making friends can be hard.
How do you make a friend?

What if you are shy,
or you just don't know how to make a friend,
or even how to start?

Maybe you can start
just by saying *Hi!* with your eyes,
or maybe you can just say something nice
to a kid you want to be friends with.

Maybe you can ask that kid
what he or she is doing,
and then you can ask
if you can join in.

Maybe if you have a ball,
or a treat or a game,
you can offer to share that
with the kid you want to be friends with.

Hey, you have to be a little brave,
and do a little work
to make a friend, OK?

Is a friend forever?

Sometimes things change with a friend,
even with a best friend.

Maybe you have a best friend,
somebody who you really like
and somebody who you think really likes you.

But then maybe one day
your best friend doesn't want to play with you,
or even to talk with you.

Did that ever happen to you?

Maybe your best friend
won't even tell you *why*
he or she doesn't want to play
or even talk to you.

Ouch! That can hurt your feelings, right?

What can you do about that one?

What if one day your friend
becomes mean to you,
and you don't understand why?

Maybe you can just ask your friend,
*"Hey, did I do something wrong to you,
or did I say something wrong?"*

Maybe your friend will tell you
what is bothering him or her.
Then maybe you can talk about it
and maybe you can become friends again.

But what if your friend
doesn't even want to talk about it?
Maybe then you can ask your teacher,
or another friend to help you talk it over.

Sometimes a kid is having problems,
and it really has nothing to do with you.

Well, maybe then it's just time to play alone,
or with some other kids —
until that other friend comes back around.

What if there is a group of kids
who are always together,
like they think they're real popular, right?

What if you want to be part of that group?

Maybe you can just go over
and ask if you can play with them.

Maybe those kids say *OK!*
and then you all play together —
and you let other kids join in too.

But maybe those kids act mean,
like they *don't* want to play with you.

Ouch! That can hurt too!

Well, maybe then you really don't need
to be part of that group, right?

Or, are you one of the kids in a group
that is mean to other kids?

What if there is a kid who is always fighting?

What if there is a kid who is a bully,
or a kid who is always teasing,
or telling other kids not to play with you,
or a kid who tries to hurt other kids,
or who is always making trouble?

Can you be friends with that kid?

What if a kid never tries,
or what if a kid doesn't talk to anybody?

Can you be friends with that kid?

What if a kid never shares,
or if a kid is always bragging, or lying?

Can you be friends with kids
that are having some kind of problems?

Should you try?

What if a kid always looks unhappy,
or if he never laughs?

What if a kid is always picking his nose,
or if he forgets to cover his mouth
when he coughs?

What if a kid is in a wheelchair,
or if he wears raggedy clothes?

What if a kid does annoying stuff,
like talking out of turn, or disturbing others,
or pushing to the front of the line,
or if he just does unusual stuff
like flapping his hands around?

What if a kid is slow in reading,
or is doing poorly with his school work?

What if a kid has a different skin color,
or is from a different religion than you are?

Wow! Sometimes you may think
that it's just easier to be friends
with people who look and act
the same as you and your other friends, right?

Really? Is having a friend
who is just the same as you
and your other friends,
the only way to have a friend?

Can you have a friend
who is different than you,
who looks and acts differently
than you and your other friends?

Maybe you can learn a lot from a friend
who is different than you.

Maybe a friend who is different than you
can show you a new way to think,
or even a new way to feel.

Maybe a friend who is different than you
can show you a new way to see things,
or a new way to understand things.

Maybe a friend who is different than you
can even show you *better* ways
to see and understand things!

Most of our friends are people
but maybe we can have other friends also.

Did you ever have an *imaginary* friend?

An imaginary friend is somebody
that only *you* can see or talk to —
but why would anybody
have an imaginary friend?

Maybe a kid has an imaginary friend
because he or she is really lonely,
or there is something going on
and that kid doesn't know
how to tell anybody else about it.

Or maybe a kid has an imaginary friend
just because he or she has a great imagination!

It's OK to have an imaginary friend,
and it's OK to share your imaginary friend
with somebody else too.

There are lots of other friends we can also have!

Usually our Mom and Dad are our best friends,
and also our families are our friends.
Maybe your pet dog or cat is your friend
because they always play with you,
and you can cuddle with them and feel safe.

Maybe the earth is our friend
because it gives us its beautiful rivers,
and lakes and oceans,
and mountains and forests.

And maybe we can also be friends
with the earth by keeping it clean,
and not leaving litter on the ground,
or putting garbage into the water.

Maybe you have a friend
who is special in your religion.

Maybe you can be your own friend
by doing good things for yourself
like eating healthy food, getting enough sleep,
learning to read and write —
and even just by being nice to other people!

And maybe you even have a friend
that you have never met before —
but wait, how could that be?

What is a friend?

A friend is somebody
who helps you when you need help,
and a friend is somebody
who you can also help.

A friend is somebody that you can trust,
and somebody that you can share
important stuff with.

A friend is somebody who shows you
how to be a better person.

And, a real friend is forever.

Look around for a minute —
wouldn't it be great
if we could *all* be friends?